STORY NUMBER 1

STORY NUM

A Harlin Quist Book

Published by Harlin Quist, Incorporated.
Library of Congress Catalog Card: 78-70567.

BER 1 BY EUGENE IONESCO
WITH PICTURES
BY JOEL NAPRSTEK

ISBN: 0-8252-8169-5 for the paperback,

0-8252-8171-7 for the hardcover.
Translated by Calvin K. Towle.

Designed by Patrick Couratin.
First printing. Printed in the U.S.A.

Josette is thirty-three months old, and she is already a big girl. One morning, just as she does every morning, Josette walks with quick little steps to the door of her parents' bedroom. She tries to open the door, pushing it like a little dog. Then she loses patience and calls out, waking her parents — who pretend not to hear.

On this particular day, papa and mama are

tired. Last night they went to the theatre; then, after the theatre, to a nightclub. And now they feel lazy. And it is not good for parents to feel that way...

The maid loses her patience too. She opens the door of the bedroom and says: "Good morning, madame. Good morning, sir. Here is your morning newspaper, here are the post-cards you have received, here is your coffee with cream and sugar, here is your fruit juice, here are your rolls, here is your toast, here is your butter, here is your orange marmalade, here is your strawberry jam, here are your fried eggs, here is your ham, and here is your little girl."

The parents feel sick, because (to tell the truth) after the nightclub they went to another restaurant. They don't want to drink their

coffee, they don't want the toast, they don't want the rolls, they don't want the ham, they don't want the eggs, they don't want the orange marmalade, they don't want their fruit juice, they don't want the strawberry jam (which isn't strawberry anyway, but more orange).

"Give all that to Josette," says papa to the maid, "and bring her back to us after she has eaten."

The maid takes the little girl in her arms. Josette howls. But because she is greedy, she consoles herself in the kitchen by eating mama's marmalade, papa's jam, and both her parents' rolls. Then she drinks the fruit juice.

"Oh, what a little monster!" says the maid. "You have a belly as big as your eyes."

To help the little girl (so that she will not be sick), the maid drinks the coffee and eats the

eggs and the ham – and also some rice with milk which had been left from the night before.

During this time, papa and mama fall back to sleep and begin to snore. But not for long. The maid brings Josette back to the bedroom.

"Papa, Jacqueline –" says Josette, "Jacqueline ate your ham."

"That's all right," says papa.

"Papa," says Josette, "tell me a story."

And while mama sleeps (because she is exhausted from having celebrated too much), papa tells Josette a story.

"Once there was a little girl named Jacqueline."

"Like Jacqueline?" asks Josette.

"Yes," says papa, "but this wasn't Jacqueline. Jacqueline was a little girl. She had a mama who was named Mrs. Jacqueline. Her

papa was named Mr. Jacqueline. The little Jacqueline had two sisters who were both named Jacqueline, and two boy cousins who were named Jacqueline, and two girl cousins who were named Jacqueline, and an aunt and an uncle who were named Jacqueline.

The uncle and the aunt named Jacqueline had some friends named Mr. and Mrs. Jacqueline, who had a little girl named Jacqueline

and a little boy named Jacqueline. The little girl had three dolls named Jacqueline, Jacqueline, and Jacqueline. The little boy had a friend named Jacqueline, and some wooden horses named Jacqueline, and some toy soldiers named Jacqueline.

One day little Jacqueline, with her papa Jacqueline, her little brother Jacqueline, and her mama Jacqueline, went to the park.

There they met their friends the Jacquelines, with their little girl Jacqueline, their little boy Jacqueline, with the dolls Jacqueline, Jacqueline and Jacqueline."

As papa is telling the story to Josette, the maid comes in. "You are going to drive the child crazy, sir," she says.

"Jacqueline, are you going shopping?" says Josette to the maid. (Remember, the maid is also named Jacqueline.) Josette goes off to run some errands with the maid.

Papa and mama fall asleep again because they are very tired. The night before, they went to a restaurant, to the theatre, again to a restaurant, to a nightclub, then again to a restaurant.

Josette goes into a shop with the maid, where she meets a little girl who is with her parents. Josette says. "Want to play with me? What's your name?"

The little girl says: "My name is Jacqueline."

"I know," says Josette. "Your papa is named Jacqueline, your mama is named Jacqueline, your little brother is named Jacqueline, your

doll is named Jacqueline, your grandpapa is named Jacqueline, your wooden horse is named Jacqueline, your house is named Jacqueline, your little chamber pot is named Jacqueline..."

Then the grocer, the grocer's wife, the little girl's mother, and all the customers in the store turn toward Josette and look at her with big, frightened eyes.

"It's nothing," the maid says calmly. "Don't be upset. These are just the silly stories her papa tells her."